BEAUTIFUL INNOCENCE
STOLEN

BEAUTIFUL INNOCENCE STOLEN

Healing from sexual abuse

NAKISKA J

AIMVH Books and Publishing

Contents

Intro

Healing is an essential process for your recovery from sexual abuse. To move forward with life, one must gain inner healing. You made it to a point in life where you have sought deliverance, but your pain still lives in your mind. The memories taunt your emotions with that harsh terror. It's affecting your viewpoint of yourself, your relationships, and taking a toll on your life. Journey with me from a space of pain to an area of freeing yourself through inner healing. It won't feel good initially, but you need it. It is time for you to find yourself, become whole, and step into your full healing. Ask yourself, "Am I ready?"

Releasing the pain: Tell your story

Journey with me as I tell my story. While reading, think about your story of where your pain began. Think of the moment where you first felt unprotected. My moment of feeling unprotected began at the first occurrence of being molested.

My story begins as a little girl around the age of four or five. I woke up in a dark living room, staring around a pitch dark room from a queen blue air bed looking for my older brother. To my surprise, the face staring back at me was not that of my brother. He asked me to lay down, but I told him "no." I asked him, "Where is my brother?" "In the restroom," he responded. "He is not allowed to come out of the bathroom," he said. I got up and walked from the dark living room into a lit hallway. The restroom door was cracked open, so I knocked on the door; no answer. I waited a few minutes before opening the door to find an empty bathroom.

I was afraid to go back into the living room, so I peeked into the boy's room to find my older brother asleep in a bottom bunk. I attempted to awaken him with a tap on his shoulder, but he was sound asleep. That night I chose to break my grandmother's rule for no girls in the boy's room. I balled up behind my brother and fell sound asleep. I decided not to be molested that night.

My molestation went on for approximately two years. I felt alone during this time. I was trying to stop the situation, but no one was trying to help me. Each night before bed, I would pray to the Lord for my abuser not to bother me. Sometimes my prayer was answered, and I would feel relieved and full of gratitude. Other times disappointment would settle in as I would awaken to my abuser on top of me or me waking up to locate my panties.

There were many nights where I found myself not so lucky. The experiences spark the first time of my feeling like I did not have a voice. From those moments, I was forced to learn how to keep things to myself. My coping mechanism for guarding myself began here from my childhood.

I can vividly recall that morning waking up hearing one of Baby Face's songs playing loud in the room from the radio sitting on the dresser. I was in the boy's room again. This time, I was lying in my abuser's bed. I looked around for my panties to put them back on. I was frustrated and fed up with him molesting me. I had worked up the nerve to finally inform my grandmother about what had been happening to me. I told my abuser I was planning to let my grandmother know what he had been doing that morning. His response to me was, "go ahead. She will not believe you". With tears pouring from my eyes, I told him, "she would." He looked at me and, with a demonic laugh, said, "okay." After locating my panties and placing them back on, I ran out of his bed into the hallway where my grandmother was doing the morning wake up call for breakfast. I ran up to her with great excitement to finally tell her what my cousin had been doing to me, and she stopped me. She told me to shut my mouth and proceeded to question me as to why I was coming out of the boy's room. Her response to me came as a shock because she said she knew that I was sleeping in the boy's room when I was not supposed to and that she finally caught me. The next thing I recall was her whooping me with a switch. She never heard my reasoning; I never had a chance to tell her my story.

She had stolen my opportunity of freedom from molestation. That moment drove me into a mental place of solitude. I could not understand why I was being chastised for something that was not my fault. I began keeping my feelings locked up, and at each occurrence, silently crying as the molestation continued.

On another occasion, I remember it was a beautiful sunny day during the summertime. My cousin was babysitting my siblings, a little cousin, and myself. We all asked to go outside to play because we were bored in the house. Everyone was allowed to go out except me. I felt a dreadful feeling in the pit of my stomach when he said it. I asked him why I could not go outside, and he told me he had to punish me because he heard I was misbehaving.

He proceeded to walk into the "girls room" and said I knew the routine. He told me to pull down my pants and panties as he closed the bedroom door. I hesitated as the tears began to roll down my face. He told me to hurry up because he had to get outside to watch the others. I finally pulled them down to the floor, and he laid me on the larger bed in the middle of the room. I watched him pull down his pants while proceeding to pull out his penis as I cried, begging him not to do it. He got on top of me and inserted himself inside of me. It did not hurt me physically because he had already violated me often, but emotionally he was destroying me in ways that would later affect me in adulthood. Once he ejaculated, he wiped me off with a wet rag and told me to put my clothes back on. He then told me not to say anything, so I went outside to play as if nothing wrong had taken place in the house. When asked what took so long, he told everyone he was waiting for me to finish using the restroom.

I never attempted to tell anyone else about this horrible thing that was happening to me. My mother finally picked me up one day and took me back home with her, and I felt relieved that I was finally being rescued from sexual abuse by my teenage cousin. To my surprise, however, what was being done to me was not hidden. Everyone that lived in my grandparent's house had some awareness of the molestation or knew I was waking up in my cousin's bed.

One of my adult cousins just decided to speak up for me because she grew tired of my abuse. My parents did not prosecute my abuser. Often I would wonder in my adulthood if I should report him. I often wondered how many others had he molested.

Tell your story: Part two

There were other occurrences of an attempt to molest me by two other older cousins at later ages in my childhood, and a baby sitters son once fondled me, but I made sure not to stay in a place alone with them to ensure they went no further. My fear of older men increased in my younger age, and I often wondered why I was a target for pedophiles.

As I grew into adulthood, the occurrence of sexual abuse had followed me. Both encounters took place in college weeks apart from each other. The first occurrence took place by an old friend I had reconnected with from age 13. He was about six years older than me. I was reconnected with him via telephone from a mutual acquaintance that happened to be my cousin. I invited him to my home, but he was not supposed to be coming alone. It was supposed to be a group of his family and myself hanging together.

For some reason, I never felt comfortable having him in my home alone, so I tried to get anyone I could to come to hang out with us. I called my younger brother, one of my older cousins that lived in the same city, and I even reached out to my ex-boyfriend at the time. However, no one came over. In the earlier portion of the day we hung out, he showed me pictures of his daughter and played board games. Then things took a turn. I went to lock the front door, and he walked up behind me with a lighter in hand, held it close to my hair, and said, "I can set you on fire in here, and no one would know he did it."

I never felt so terrified for my life ever. The only thing I could think about was I want to get out of this alive and unharmed. He looked at me and laughed, and went to the restroom. I was not sure how to respond. I did not call anyone because I was afraid he would attempt to harm me seriously. After coming from the restroom, he grabbed me as I walked into my bedroom and forced himself on me. I kept saying "no," but he would not stop. For a brief moment, I felt like that helpless little girl all over again. I managed to maneuver him out of me and told him to leave.

I immediately showered while crying and locked myself in the bedroom. When I awakened the next morning, the rapist was still in my home. I was a sociology major in college, and we had recently discussed how police officers treat cases when the woman knows the attacker. I didn't want to feel incriminated, so another attacker got away. I did not call the cops. He left my home that morning, and I never heard from him or saw him again.

The last occurrence took place two weeks later. My ex-boyfriend came over wanting to make up with me. He was 13 years older than me. My relationship with him was not healthy because he was a womanizer. I told him about the incident, and he became furious. He was upset with me and accused me of allowing another man to have sex with me. After I told him about the sexual assault, he asked to have sex with me, and I told him I did not want to. He became even more furious, bent me over on the bed, held my hands, and proceeded to insert himself into my anus. I hollered out and screamed for him to leave. He said he would be the first for everything with me and left my home. I continued dealing with him after the incident; he apologized and told me his feelings in the manner. My feelings towards him became numb, however. I called him for rides to work until I could get my vehicle running and left him alone ultimately. With both encounters, I felt like they were my fault in a way. I felt like I should have done more, I should have reported them, but for some reason, I didn't. That thing of not telling and allowing a sexual abuser to get away had followed me into my adulthood—a cycle of unhealthy learned behavior and trauma.

Coping After Trauma

Many times we develop negative coping responses to sexual trauma. We innately adapt to ways that may not necessarily be good for our overall health. Some negative coping responses include withdrawing from people emotionally, suppressing memories, self-blame, drugs, alcohol, and more. Those mechanisms may have helped you get through the trauma of sexual abuse. However, the best way to heal from any traumatic experience is to allow for healthy grieving—no blaming yourself, not hating the person, not carrying this significant burden throughout life.

The best start to your inner healing is to start your healing process. Accept what happened, know it's not your fault, and understand it will be a process that you may not be able to get through completely by yourself. The best thing I could ever do for myself was seek a spiritual counselor to help me address the feelings I suppressed while offering tools and guidance to get through my coping process healthily. Believe it or not, healing first begins when you share your story.

I believe I went through several processes in my coping. When my parents first asked me about my molestation, they asked if my cousin hurt me, and I told them, "no." I never shared details of occurrences because my parents never asked. After settling in with my mom again, I went through the phase of suppressing all memories.

Until the age of eight or nine, I did not recall the molestation. In my mind, nothing ever happened to me. My mother did her best not to have my cousin come around our home for years to ensure he did not molest me again. I always had a fear of him as a child but never recalled the specific occurrences.

The first time I ever saw him again was around the age of nine. He was in town visiting with one of our other cousins. My siblings and I were over for a sleepover. The cousin who molested me was allowed to visit that particular family member home while I was there, but he could not stay overnight due to what took place when I was younger.

After the suppression phase came a great fear of teenage boys that were high school or college age. I would cringe up with anxiety whenever I was in the presence of a guy in that age group. I can recall one memory of me walking home from school. When I was in the sixth grade, my older brother left school without me, so I had to walk home alone. My fear was not walking home by myself; my fear was passing a house up the street from the apartment complex we lived in, where a group of older guys would hang out. I remember praying for someone to walk with me to feel safe walking past that home, and my prayers were answered.

I ran into a young lady who did not want to walk home alone, so we walked and talked together. As we approached the home, I recall the anxiety and fear that almost overtook me at that moment. The only thought I had was that I did not want to be raped or molested again. I felt the tears starting to fold from my eyes as my mother drove up looking for me. She was upset and fussed at me because she saw the boys on the porch, and she was afraid for me because of the molestation. She scolded me for not walking home with my brother. Of course, I became angry with my older brother because he did not wait to walk home with me.

The first time I ever shared my story about being molested, I was thirteen years old. It was a beautiful sunny day outside, and I played on the swing at a park up the street from my grandparent's home in the country during the summer. I began to share my story of molestation with two of my female cousins while playing. One of them informed me of her occurrence as well. I was shocked but also felt an incredible world of relief because I thought at that moment that I was no longer alone because someone else shared my same experience. I did encourage her to tell an adult, and my journey of coping began that day.

I was not going into details about what had happened, but it was a start to my healing and my cousin's healing because she could share with someone. I would randomly come across people around my age throughout my young adult years and be compelled to tell my story, only for them to open up with me. I was now beginning to accept the molestation, open up about it, and start my proper grieving process. I had to learn to cope with my feelings after sexual trauma more healthily.

Forgiving is a key

They say forgiveness is for you and not the other person. Speaking from experience, I can say this is true. Holding on to unforgiveness holds you bound. It can cause you unwanted health problems, create mental health issues, keep you tied to depression, and merely unhealed. To get to a place of inner healing, the first person you must forgive is self. Yes, this is the hard one. We can often displace blame onto ourselves unnecessarily. Start a process of forgiving everyone you feel contributed directly or indirectly to your sexual abuse experience. I know for many a hard part may be confronting an abuser, and for this one, I will say seek Christ first. Pray regarding your own heart towards them and whether it is necessary for your healing process to speak with that person or not.

Sometimes letters are the best way to release what we want to say. However you decide to map out your process for your road to forgiveness, just start. Keep a realistic mindset and know that not everyone will accept fault or blame regarding the situation, which is okay. Remember, forgiveness is for you to release yourself so that you can move forward within your life.

The last occurrence I had where I allowed myself to be in a private space to talk to my cousin who molested me was in my early 20's. During that time, I grew into my spiritual gifts and firmly focused on developing in the Lord. I never discussed what he had done to me with him out of fear of him saying the wrong thing or him not feeling remorse. I genuinely wanted to see him change his life for the better. At that time, I spoke with him regarding getting into the church, and he shared how he started going to church, and things were shifting for him in his life when he did so. Knowing him changing his life and following Christ could positively impact other cousins' lives that looked up to him made me feel happy and not hateful.

During my healing journey, I had to acknowledge the beginning of my sexual trauma when my pain of not being protected began and start my forgiveness process. I had many to forgive: my father for abandoning us, my mother for not taking us with her initially, my deceased grandmother, who blamed me, aunts, cousins, and everyone directly or indirectly involved. We tend to think healing comes overnight, and in some forms, it can, but when we walk around harboring unforgiveness for years, it takes a process for uprooting that pain to walk in forgiveness.

If you are like me, you thought being able to talk about your sexual abuse meant complete healing or the lack of not talking about it. Or maybe you believed because you can now speak to this person, you are okay. Until one day, you find yourself projecting those fears of what happened to you onto your partner. Maybe you are a person who started using sex as a way of control or as a source of stress release. No, still not you? Perhaps you are the person that watches pornography to masturbate. Or your sexual lifestyle is a direct impact of your traumatic sexual abuse. The list can go on. Until one day, you find yourself with that feeling of discomfort regarding that person.

True forgiveness means forgiving and, in some cases forgetting if it is not going to do you or anyone you come across justice in being recalled. Remember, if God uses your story to help someone else see what a conqueror looks like, then the memories must begin to no longer cause you discomfort to share.

I started my forgiveness process ten years ago, and here I am still trying to complete it because I stopped. Do not be like me; keep going until you see the finished product. Because I chose to complete my process, I can now write this book, which was supposed to be published two years ago. Remember, forgiving is freeing you. One thing that has been helping me to forgive truly is to stand on scripture regarding forgiving others. I am listing three, but there are several that you can search that relate to forgiving.

Bear with each other and forgive one another. If any of you has a grievance against someone. Forgive as the Lord forgave you. Colossians 3:13

And when you stand praying, if you hold anything against anyone, forgive them so that your father in heaven may forgive you your sins. Mark 11:25

You Lord are forgiving and good, abounding in love to all who call to you. Psalm 86:5

A story that stands out to me regarding forgiveness is the biblical story regarding Job. God could not release the blessings of restoration he had awaiting Job until he first forgave the people he held unforgiveness with. It was not Job's fault for the occurrences experienced, but he had to release them to get better. As you continue reading, make a written list of everyone you have not entirely forgiven. Your sexual abuser or abusers should be listed first and continue from there.

After making your list start name by name and say out loud, "I forgive you, and I release you this day," and insert what you forgive them for. Some people you are going to have to make direct phone calls to for relationship restoration, others may be letters sent, others may be in the form of a prayer for forgiveness. However you are being led to obtaining your release, "LET GO." Now is your time to finally get free. Feel your shackles releasing as you speak your forgiveness. Release them so you can receive your blessing of inner healing.

Getting in front of fear

Now that you have gone through this process of recalling and sharing the memories about sexual abuse, now you must move past those images. As I was completing my internal healing process, I came across a Pastor's Facebook service regarding entering into the "promised land." In this series, he discussed the topic of fear of rebuking fear because it will always exist, but praying for courage to get in front of fear. Why am I mentioning fear here, you ask? I mention fear because it will begin speaking loud during this next phase.

It will have you thinking you are too far along to be healed or trick you into thinking you do not require additional healing. It will have you afraid to revisit memories you have suppressed. It will have you frightened to confront those you need to forgive. It will tell you people are going to reject you. It will place negative thoughts in your mind to cause you to step back from complete healing.

It's perfectly normal to feel the discomfort of fear, but do not allow it to drive you. Get in front of your fears. You deserve this, and it is yours to have if you want it. Get control of your life this day. If we conquer fear, there is nothing on earth we would not be able to do. Let getting to full inner healing be your first thing fear cannot stop. It does not matter if your sexual abuse took place 50 years ago, 20 years ago, one year ago, or yesterday. It is not too late.

Of course, the longer the period that had elapsed between when the abuse took place and now, understand it will be a process you will have to dedicate to completing yourself. Find someone to help hold you accountable. Some days will be more challenging than others, but this is where you conquer fear by outlasting it. A few scriptures you will want to stand on regarding conquering fear. I am listing four, but there are several more to seek out that pertain to you.

> He will never leave you nor forsake you. Do not be afraid; do not be discouraged. Deuteronomy 31:8

> Do not fear for I have redeemed you; I have called you by name; you are mine. Isaiah 43:1

> The Lord is my rock, my fortress, and my deliverer. Psalm 18:2

> For God has not given us a spirit of fear but of power, love, and a sound mind. 2 Timothy 1:7

When I think of conquering fear, I think of the biblical story regarding David and Goliath. I love this story because it shows proof of holding a real faith in our Lord in Heaven for overcoming fear. I love the point in the story when David finds himself face to face with Goliath. He looks Goliath in his face and tells him he will slay him just as he killed the beasts before him because God is with him.

You have to think this way in regards to overcoming the trauma associated with the sexual abuse that happened to you. Release the ownership of it. Yes, it happened, it was a horrible experience, but it is not yours. It was a sad event that happened to you, but it is not a gift to call your own. It is an occurrence that God can and will heal you from if you allow it. Today, face your fear from sexual abuse in the face, and tell it, " you shall destroy its roots today in the power of your Lord and Savior Jesus the Christ."

Destroying false images

Satan will use images in our mind to give us false perceptions, force the memories of traumatic experiences to drive you into depression, make you think drugs or drinking is helping you to forget what happened. The truth is, the false imagery is causing you to stay trapped. To fully heal from your sexual abuse, you must change how you perceive the events of your sexual trauma..

If you continue to hold on to the negative images regarding your molestation and sexual abuse, then you can never reach full inner healing. For some of you, your false image may be of how you see yourself. Know you are wonderfully, fearfully made. You are a conqueror. You are worthy to truly be loved the correct way, by the right person. There is more to you than the sexualization of your body, which your sexual abuser forced upon you. You are beautiful, or you are handsome. You have to find yourself.

For me, my false imagery started in how I viewed relationships. As a little girl, I read many fairy tale books of princes rescuing the damsel in distress and her living happily ever after. I had a false image against black men because of the abuse and watching other black men my mother dated mistreating her. This imagery later grew into all men " being dogs" after bad relationships with men as I grew into an adult. I took these types of false images into relationships, and with these false images, I turned away good men or mistreated the good ones and allowed the wrong ones to mistreat me.

The truth is, sexual abuse can help shape how we view relationships later in life. It can draw you to the wrong types and cause you to run from the right kind. As I entered into my internal healing process and began tracking the kinds of relationships I have had or the lack of, I realized they were all driven by when I was molested as a kid. I formed the wrong image about sex and what it means for two people to come together. I soon realized how controlling my counterparts and disassociating from them during my sexual encounters were all driven back to that occurrence when my cousin sexually abused me as a form of punishment.

Take a moment to think about your dating relationships and how your sexual abuse has driven them. Can you see the pattern yet? These are the images that you must break. I was able to view sex as something I should wait for until marriage because it is sacred. I should not be withdrawn from it because it is an emotional experience you share with someone as they share with you, and I want to share this moment in marriage.

Ironically, as much as I feared older guys as a child, as an adult, that's all I dated. I dated a guy my age once, and that relationship lasted for a month tops. My most extended-term relationships were with men eight to 13 years older than myself. Sadly, those relationships were not the healthiest, but I was drawn to them stemming from childhood trauma. I allowed them to force sex upon me unwillingly due to the imagery placed there when my abuser would force himself on me, and it left me with a feeling of helplessness. I felt like I had to do it, not knowing I was submitting to an emotion tied to helplessness.

I also formulated images about people directly and indirectly. I blamed them for what happened to me throughout my years. To see those people positively after forgiving them, I had to understand their back story. With my first sexual abuser, I later learned he was a victim of abuse as a kid, so he was projecting what was done to him on to me. However, this does not excuse his wrong actions. It helped me seek my forgiveness and pray that they, one day, find the healing I am now obtaining today. I understand many things in my family took place that many did not address. So their responses to my molestation were formulated from their own life experiences. By changing my perception about them, I gained empathy for them to forgive them better and not hold them to my past when they have their histories to give account for.

The reality of life is no matter how much we want to be people's judges and condemn for their wrong actions, we all have an account-ability to God on judgment day. It is not your duty to ensure your abuser, your parents, or whoever was directly or indirectly involved pays for what they did or forcing them to feel accountable. It is not our place to hold a person to their past when they have gone to God themselves for their own atonement. Release yourself from that false image. Let God obtain justice for you. Your only job is to release them in forgiveness and move forward with your life positively.

In dealing with false images, we have to destroy the images formed from our sexual abuse forced upon our children. When my daughter was born, I feared leaving her around her father, simply because of what happened to me. It drove me into becoming a very overprotective mother. I did not trust any man or boys around my daughter. I have a best friend who has sons, and when we would go to his home, I would make my daughter sit with me when all she wanted to do was watch them play video games. In my mind, I was protecting my daughter from what happened to me.

It is perfectly normal to want to protect your kids, but when fear drives you not to allow your child to be loved by the other parent whose only desire is to protect your child like you, it is not healthy. That same mindset can cause marriages to fail because you are following a false image. Set healthy boundaries for your children, teach them the important things about what sexual abuse is, and look like, but do not continue to allow what happened to you to be a driving force of you trying to protect your child from people who would never hurt them.

A favorite scripture that comes to mind regarding getting rid of false images and changing your perception in regards to inner healing and past sexual abuse is:

> Casting down imaginations, and every high
> thing that exalteth itself against the knowledge of
> God, and bringing into captivity every thought to
> the obedience
> of Christ. 2 Corinthians 10:5

As you journey into full inner healing, make a list of images and perceptions driven by the trauma from being sexually abused. Think about how it causes you to see yourself, dating prospects, maybe a spouse, your children, men in general, women in general, how it shapes your sexual experiences, and whatever other ways come to mind. Now, think about ways of changing those perceptions and viewpoints that are projecting as negative images. If you need a counselor to help you at this point, get whatever positive help to keep you moving towards your inner healing.

Re-building Self-Esteem

You are now ready to rediscover who you are; the point where you are now the focus. The first question you need to ask yourself is, "What is my worth?" When you begin to discover you are of value, you can start building your self-worth after the traumas of sexual abuse.

You have been torn down for years, and now you must be built up. The word rebuilding reminds me of a home being remodeled. Sometimes a home has to be torn completely down and rebuilt from the ground up. At first, that home looks rough. There is debris from torn down walls, flooring, and cabinetry. As the house is being rebuilt, it starts taking shape until you get to the finished product. Once the construction is complete, that home is gorgeous. You no longer see the broken pieces, just a home that looks nothing like its building process. You must see yourself as that home, being built up and beautified from the inside out. The scars and brokenness you endured from your sexual abuse is now being reconstructed into your purpose.

You are now reshaping yourself. This means seeing yourself as a warrior and victorious because though you came out with bruises and scars, it did not kill you. That means there is a purpose to be born from that pain. You are stronger than you have given yourself credit. In rebuilding your self-esteem, you have to price your value high. In this, you must destroy the self-sabotaging thoughts that are there only to steal from you. Start each day with positive affirmations. The more you speak out loud to yourself, the more you will begin to believe in yourself and start building yourself up.

During this process of building my self-esteem, I had to begin each day with positive affirmations. I started saying small prayers or reading scripture to help uplift my spirit to focus on seeing the good in me instead of focusing on what I could not control. In this process, you must take a holistic approach (mind, body, soul).

Change comes through repetition. Speaking positively to you is a must to help you become the best you. Find positive quotes, use scripture, or say positive things to yourself in a mirror and throughout your day to help rebuild your thoughts. When you feel those negative thoughts or feelings come up, those prayers and affirmations are your tools to counteract those thoughts. The more you reaffirm your beliefs, the more productive you will start to see yourself becoming. As you build yourself up mentally, you will begin feeling great about yourself daily, you will find motivation, and you will start discovering passion. The more you tell yourself you can, you will. You will begin to see you can conquer all.

In building your mind, you will begin to develop your body. The things that you once used to harm your body, you will want to stop. As you build your mental value, you will begin to value your body. The desire for drugs, promiscuous behavior, poor eating habits, eating disorders, alcohol, cutting, and all negative things that once brought you gratification, you will begin to change. Now that you see you are of great value, you will want your body to be healthy. You will want to exercise more and take care of yourself. Sometimes you have to make yourself look good on the outside to help you feel good on the inside.

You can't forget building your soul when creating positive self-esteem or, should we say, self-worth. Your soul is what connects your mind and body. Building your soul comes through prayer and meditation. To discover who you are comes with having a connection with the Heavenly Father. Through Him, your soul can be cleansed and built up in ways we are incapable of building ourselves.

The more you build your self-esteem, the more you will want to surround yourself with positive-minded people, you will discover an inner joy, and you will begin to feel good about who you are. The scars you gained from your experience of sexual abuse and molestation will slowly start to heal day by day. Some days will be better than others, but as long as you keep building, you will get to that process where your scars no longer define you.

A scripture to keep in mind when you are defining your self-worth is John 3:16:

> For God so loved the world, that He gave his only begotten Son, that whoever believes in Him should not perish, but have everlasting life. God did not send His Son into the world to condemn it the world, but in order that the world might be saved through Him.

Knowing the price has been paid for, you should let you know you are valued highly. Your sexual abuser may have taken from you in those moments of sexual abuse, but now it is time to take you back. A few daily declarations and affirmations you can make to yourself can be:

I am strong.
I am victorious.
I am beautiful.
I am worthy.
I am more than a conqueror.
I can do all things through Christ.
I am not an accident.
I am somebody.
I can get through this.

Take more time for yourself, discover yourself. Grow and build you.

Rebuilding Your Identity

Trauma such as molestation and sexual abuse can create a false identity in a person. According to Webster dictionary, identity is the distinguishing character or personality of an individual. Pain often will cause us to have insecurities within ourselves and others. Knowing who you are and growing in that portion of you will bring forth more significant inner healing.

Trauma will distract you from the divinity of purpose at times or cause you not to walk in full purpose. Knowing who you are and becoming that person will help you develop a sense of inner peace and joy that any person or situation cannot steal. To inwardly heal, your identity is a must to discover.

I found my identity getting lost in what I wanted to do and whom I wanted to be. I spent most of my life trying to be and do what I felt my spiritual leaders wanted, family wanted, employers wanted, an image that I falsely created, all while losing me. After losing my job in March of 2019, I decided to start building for myself. November 2020 marked the highlight of my finding myself thoroughly after coming out of a spiritually exhausting dating re-lationship. I decided enough was enough. This moment marked the last time I would allow someone to take my joy and self-worth from me. My counselor has been great in allowing God to use her to give me just the tools I need to rediscover myself.

One of the great exercises she gave me was to write down and answer two questions; Who am I? and; What is my purpose? Answering these questions honestly helped in transforming my mind to focus more on me. Rebuilding my identity caused me to put more emphasis on myself without apologies. It also forced me to make closer analyses of the people in my circle. I had to realize those who were encouraging me to be the person I want to be from those pulling me to who they wanted me to be.

During this time, make time for yourself. Take time to heal for you. Don't put so much focus into others that you neglect you. I am starting to take 45 minutes a day for time to myself to do absolutely nothing. It was another great suggestion by my counselor. It was something I never thought of doing. I put so much time into being a mother, being a girlfriend, being a daughter, being an author, and the list goes on that I never took time to breathe and be me.

When healing from the trauma of sexual abuse, discovering you and settling into your own identity helps with your healing. Discover your purpose and fulfill it because it makes you happy. That feeling that you have been running from or avoiding that is connected to your divinity is what you should be seeking. Much prayer and supplication will help you to discover your true identity.

Overcoming Anxiety

Ever woke up at 2 am from a sound sleep all because you cannot catch your breath. That horrid sensation of feeling like something is sitting in the center of your chest, and you are continually trying to breathe. As I went through my inner healing process, I found myself in this place for four days. I went to the doctor, only to discover I was having an onset of panic attacks.

Sounds extreme, right? Yes, I thought so too. Believe it or not, sexual trauma can trigger the body to respond in many ways when it feels stressed or overwhelmed. Once I realized it was an onset of anxiety instead of that dreaded Covid, I decided to do something about it. Yes, healing from trauma like sexual abuse can trigger many-body and mental reactions. So going through this process, I took to prayer and learned how to calm myself. One tool I found valuable was meditation. Your phone has meditation apps on it. Try downloading some if you begin feeling yourself become anxious for no reason.

If you begin to tune in to your body, you can prevent an anxiety attack by changing your focus or focusing on your breathing. Again, this may not be everyone's case, but dealing with trauma and memories can trigger anxious moments. Natural things to use are essential oils within a diffuser. Sweet orange and lavender essential oils are great fragrances to have in your home for that calming effect.

Also, take time to exercise and, at minimum, get 30 minutes of outdoor time as possible. Remember, this process is about you holistically. Music is another calming tool. Try to stay away from things that would cause triggers during this process until you become stronger mentally and spiritually.

Tearing Down Inner Walls

Dealing with the years of inner walls built from sexual abuse trauma requires self-acknowledgment of them existing. When trauma occurs, the first defense is to put up emotional walls to cope with the event. How long have you been building your walls? How did it begin? These are questions you have to start with to work them down.

Emotional walls affect how we build relationships with others. Often, these walls are made to keep people from getting close to you emotionally. Emotional walls cause you to fictitiously guard yourself against feeling pain while numbing you and causing you to self isolate from others.

Take the time to think about and write down all the emotional walls you have built up for yourself over the years. Now think about how it affected relationships with family, friends, outsiders, and even dating relationships. Those walls have kept you from being loved and wholly loving. Those walls have kept you from trusting others. Those walls have kept you locked up internally, feeling alone.

My emotional walls had existed for 30 years until recently. Because of those walls, I never allowed people to get close to me. I found myself seeking excuses to push people away and shutting them out of my life, especially those I felt contributed to my latter emotional pains and griefs.

Because I know my purpose relates to the entertainment arena for singing and writing books and ultimately called to a ministry form, I knew I could not continue to allow my walls to stay up. I had to change my mindset from flight mode to fight mode.

You have to lay pride down to fix the inner parts of you while recognizing you built the walls out of circumstances due to sexual trauma. I had to start trusting myself first. Trusting myself to know I will make the best decisions for me. I had to release the walls built up from my parents as well. Those emotional walls created divisions that made it easier for me to stay away from them or keep my distance. Those walls kept me from sharing my true feelings with my parents. To overcome this, I had to begin to open up about my feelings.

I hated sharing my feelings with people because I did not trust people to handle my feelings properly. This also comes with knowing whom to communicate with and what to share with them. Opening up to my parents about my sexual abuse was not easy. I thought it would put them in a place of feeling like they allowed it by not being there, but I wanted them to be at peace, knowing it did not break me. I opened up in bits and pieces with my mom to see her reactions when discussing certain things about what happened. I have not spoken to my father regarding my sexual abuse yet, but I am working on it.

Even in dating relationships, opening up about how I truly felt about a person was very difficult. Often, I would avoid dating to avoid the emotional vulnerability of sharing my feelings with someone, in conjunction with dealing with theirs. I can look over my life and see how the emotional walls have affected my relationship with family and even church members.

When you step out to free yourself from emotional walls, you have to remember they were not formed in one day, so they will take time and effort on your part to be set free from them finally. When

I think about emotional walls, I am reminded of Jericho's wall found in the book of Joshua chapter 6 in the bible. The barrier prevented them from inhabiting the promised land.

Joshua led the Israelites with instructions to blow ram horns for six days marching around Jericho's wall with the priests, and on the seventh day, they raised a loud noise, which caused the wall to tumble down. Once down, they had to go in and destroy everything there before possessing the land and building anew.

Think of your emotional walls as hindrances to your promised land. They hinder you from true love, restrict you from friends, hinder you from healthy relationships, hinder you from inner freedom, and limit you from growing. As you remove the walls you have built, take time to pray for deliverance from those things and put your game plan in place. Write out and put into practice ways of emotionally opening up to others and yourself. Finally, getting to that place where you don't have to live life alone and no longer have to suffer from the memories alone. You can heal, you can be free, and you can allow love to come in safely.

Track your progress as you work through tearing down those inner walls. Open up to those who can help you heal in those areas as well. Just because you have lived life this way for this long does not mean you have to keep doing life that way. You are your option for new. It's going to seem scary because you will experience emotions and feelings you have never had to share. You are going to have to be vulnerable at times, and it is okay.

Understand it is a process you are in, so allow yourself the time to keep healing from your sexual abuse, but do not prolong it just because you are afraid. Free yourself and get to a mental promised land where you can be emotionally free from those walls you built from years of pain and trauma after being sexually abused.

Telling Loved Ones

Advising your loved ones about your sexual abuse will help them understand you and help your process as you grow with your family, friends, and more. Involving your close circle will create an educational moment for you to teach them and allow them into your historical world. The best way to end cycles is to inform our circle and educate them.

I informed my daughter about my molestation when she was nine years old. She asked a few questions to make sense of what I was telling her, like why they did it. She knows I keep her from around those family members to protect her from being exposed to the same experience I had.

I have made close friends aware of my sexual abuse and asked them not to feel bad or angry about the occurrence. I never seek sympathy from people when I tell them about my sexual abuse, so when informing them, I advise them that I am okay, so they do not become emotional or angry. It is okay to tell your spouse, children, siblings, and even friends about your molestation. They can even be a form of emotional support to you.

You will be surprised by the number of people you are connected closely to who have experienced the same thing you have. Telling my friends allowed them that space to share their own experiences with me. It bonded us differently because we now share a common understanding and can be one another's comfort where needed.

Dating After Sexual Abuse

Dating after trauma when unhealed looks much different than dating when you have healed or started your healing process from the trauma caused by sexual abuse. You will often find yourself caught up in unhealthy relationships before finding a healthy relationship when dealing with the emotional trauma from sexual abuse. You owe it to yourself to heal first before attempting to date. Understand and own yourself before trying to share yourself with someone else if you are single. Not starting your healing process and trying to have a healthy marriage or healthy relationship can create many difficulties for you with your partner.

My pre-healing relationships were very much unhealthy. I dated, seeking a fairy tale relationship, only to end up dating a guy who was ten years older than me in college that was emotionally abusive. I stayed as long as I did because he appealed to my sexual appetite at the time, but he was very unhealthy for me. I did not date before college out of fear of not wanting to be sexually intimate with guys.

In my relationship with the college guy, I thought we would end up married, but after three years of mistreatment, I finally decided to get out of it. I then sought sexual relationships without commitment to control my feelings, not getting caught up. Once I began to heal, I began to pull away from the unhealthy dating pattern I had developed. I began to define my value and self-worth. I began setting better standards for myself, agreeing not to be sexually intimate for spiritual aspects, guarding, and physically showing value to my body.

Now that I am obtaining inner healing, I now view my relationship standards differently than before. I no longer seek to accept just anyone for companionship. I have my standards built and only willing to commit my time to the person that is willing to reciprocate and respect those standards.

A few tips to help you venture into opening your mind to dating are being aware of red flags. Never ignore it. Be safe in your choices, and take your time. Rushing with a person can drive you into the wrong type of relationship. Demand respect by not allowing a person to go against your desires. If you say no sex before marriage, do not waste your time with someone who is continuously trying to coerce you into having sex for them to stay. Again, take your time. Get to know the person before pouring all of yourself into him or her.

If you desire certain spiritual aspects from your mate, do not date someone that does not believe as you. When you find that safe person you are compatible with, begin opening up to them, and share your story of sexual abuse with them. You should be upfront with your partner regarding your past. Be mindful of triggers that may spark anxiety when dating. Find a partner willing to go at a paste that will allow you to be comfortable with them.

Date when you are ready to do so and no sooner. You do not want to get into a relationship before you are healed from sexual trauma to create an unhealthy dating pattern. Stick with your standards, and do not settle. You deserve the best relationship for you. Do not play a victim when you have a choice not to keep playing that role. Allow them to love you when the relationship is becoming serious. Do not stay dating someone who is forcing themselves on you.

For those of you already married or engaged, communicate with your partner and ask them to help you build healthy habits within your relationship. If you are married or engaged to someone, you do not feel comfortable having around your children, evaluate if your feelings are valid. One tool I used to help me form a healthy relationship once I decided to start dating again was to change the unhealthy thought process I had regarding dating. Books and google articles are always a go-to for good and positive advice regarding building healthy relationships and what it should look like.

Now is the time to deal with those insecurities you have within yourself that you have been projecting on others. Do not stay in a place where you are projecting your pains and fears developed from your sexual abuse onto others. Set yourself free. Set your mind free. Prayer and positive affirmations are going to be your best friend in this phase.

Why do I say that? Because anytime you are trying to break free from old habits and patterns until you get all remnants of it out of your mind and spirit, it will come up in situations to distract your attention from healing if you allow it. The mind is built to be strong. The more you feed it with positivity, the greater your outcome. If you have decided to date or married, make sure you prepare yourself to share yourself and open up to your partner daily.

Here are a few unhealthy signs to look for in yourself or your partner when trying to date:

- Extreme jealousy
- Control issues
- Poor communication skills
- Social Isolation of partner
- Financial control
- Obsessive behavior

Be careful, make a list of behaviors you will not accept, hold to your standards, be willing to give what you require from a partner, be open with yourself, and share all of you when your partner is willing to share all of themselves. Pursue a relationship where the person is ready to support you and help bring out the best in you. In return, you have to reciprocate for the relationship to be healthy, and both are happy. Stay open; you can be happy and receive the love you desire.

You are Victorious

I want to encourage you. You are a survivor, and though you carry scars, you are an example of what victory looks like. You may have bruises from your sexual abuse, but that does not define who you are. I encourage you to keep seeking your inner healing daily. Inner healing is merely filling old empty spaces of hurt and pain with positive attributes and mindsets.

What was meant to kill you, you survived, we survived. Now you must become stronger from it. What was meant to cause us to abandon our real purpose, we have survived. You may have bad days, but as long as you keep going, then you are victorious. No more self-blaming, no more self-sabotaging behaviors, no more living in misery, and allowing what was out of your control to keep controlling and running your life.

As you take steps to find your inner healing from your molestation and sexual abuse, keep a journal to track your progress. Your greatest reward to yourself will be the evidence of seeing how far your progression has come daily. It is my prayer as you come to the end of your reading, that you will find comfort in knowing you are not alone. You can genuinely overcome the pains of your past.

The most challenging part of your journey will be recalling the memories of your sexual trauma, but the more you heal, the clearer your vision will become. The less hurtful the memories will become.

The more you pray, meditate, and practice positive reinforcement and affirmations, the stronger you will become. This book was not easy for me to write initially, but I am glad I did because it allowed me to complete the inner healing process that I stopped on so many years ago.

Take a physical photograph of yourself, place it on your restroom mirror so you can see it daily, and write the word victorious on it. That is who you are. Stop letting sexual abuse define your inner beauty. Your innocence was stolen but now is your chance to take it back. I encourage you to find a spiritual counselor, for some mental health counseling will be necessary to get through this process as a whole. Hold your head up high, and be the beautiful you. Please make a note of the prayer at the end of this book. I pray as you read it, you will find comfort needed in this journey of redefining yourself as you heal from sexual abuse.

Prayer for inner healing

Most gracious Father of truth, I ask you to wrap your loving arms around this reader right now. The scars and memories from their sexual abuse have stolen from them in many ways, but we know you give beauty for ashes. As this reader embarks on the journey of obtaining inner healing, strengthen their mind and heart to know they already won the victory because they are still here. Give comfort in knowing they are not a biological accident, they were born with a great purpose, and they are beautifully and wonderfully made. Fill their heart with joy and love daily, cover their mind against negative thoughts, open their eyes to see the beautiful creation you made of them that is useful to the loved ones you have placed in their life. I pray for full inner healing to this reader now in the name of Jesus the Christ. Keep them encouraged and in good spirits daily as they rediscover themselves in spirit and truth. Amen

Other Books by Author

CHURCH FROM THE EYES OF A SAINT